A Butterfly Tale

ISLAND HERITAGE™
PUBLISHING

Jennifer Fixman and Lynne Wikoff • Illustrated by Kristi Petosa-Sigel

In a beautiful Hawaiian forest, three tiny eggs rested on three Hawaiian leaves. One egg rested on a *koa* leaf, one was on *laulele*, and one lay on *māmaki*.

ISLAND HERITAGE™
PUBLISHING
A DIVISION OF THE MADDEN CORPORATION

94-411 Kōʻaki Street, Waipahu, Hawaiʻi 96797
Orders: (800) 468-2800
Information: (808) 564-8800
Fax: (808) 564-8877
islandheritage.com

ISBN NO. 1-59700-082-5
First Edition, Second Printing - 2006

After nearly a week, the three eggs began to crack. Then POOF! they hatched. Out crawled three tiny caterpillars.

"Mmm—so many delicious *koa* leaves," said Koa Caterpillar.

"Smart caterpillars eat *laulele* leaves," said Monarch Caterpillar. "Everyone knows they are best."

"You're both wrong," said Lepe-o-Hina Caterpillar. "Just looking at these *māmaki* leaves makes my mouth water."

The caterpillars argued for hours and hours about which leaves were best, until a lovely butterfly fluttered by.

"What's all the fuss?" Pulelehua Butterfly said.

"Those other caterpillars want to eat the wrong plants," said Koa. "Tell them to eat *koa* leaves."

"No," said Monarch. *"Laulele* leaves make the tastiest meals."

"No, no," said Lepe-o-Hina. "We should all eat *māmaki* leaves."

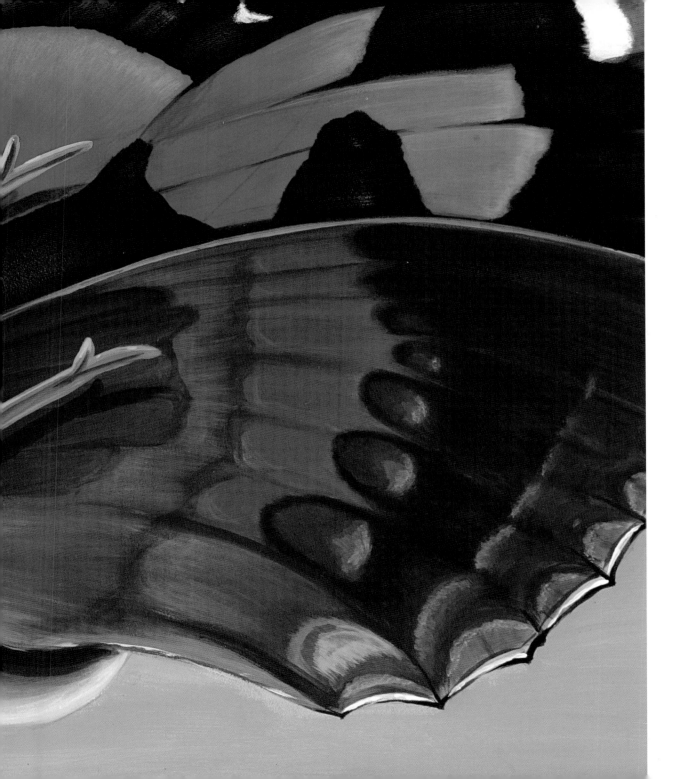

Pulelehua shook her head. "The birds are going to hear your arguing. Then they'll know where you are."

"Good, then they will agree with me," said Koa.

Pulelehua shook her head again. "No, their mouths will water. Then you'll find out what a tasty meal *really* is."

The caterpillars did not want to be a bird's dinner, but they kept arguing anyway.

They talked and yelled and screamed—and not one of them listened.

"The birds are closer than ever," Pulelehua said. "Only the spirit of *aloha* can save you now."

"What do you mean?" said Monarch. But Pulelehua was gone.

The caterpillars' empty tummies grumbled, and the birds came closer.

They shook their heads sadly.

"I guess we'll have to figure it out for ourselves," said Koa.

11

The caterpillars were quiet. They thought about being right and about the birds nearby. But most of all, they thought about friendship.

Then there was a rustle in a nearby tree.

"Was that a bird?" said Koa.

"I think it was," said Lepe-o-Hina.

"We're in big trouble now," said Monarch. "Maybe we should stop arguing and each eat our own favorite leaves."

"That idea makes my heart feel warm," said Koa. "This feeling is better than the feeling of fighting."

"My heart feels warm, too," said Monarch. "Friendship is more important than being right."

"Now we are thinking with our hearts," said Lepe-o-Hina. "That must be what Pulelehua meant by the spirit of *aloha*."

The caterpillars enjoyed the quiet company of friends as they each ate their own favorite leaves. They ate and ate and ate, and as they grew bigger and bigger, their friendship grew, too.

When their skins became too small, they crawled out of their old skins and grew new skins.

"Whee!" the caterpillars called to each other.

Pulelehua smiled as she landed on a nearby flower. "I see in your hearts that you are learning the spirit of *aloha*," she said. "When we live with *aloha*, beautiful things happen."

The caterpillars yawned as they smiled back at Pulelehua. Then they turned upside down on their favorite branches and went to sleep. And as they slept, hard cases formed around their bodies.

They weren't caterpillars anymore. Each one had become a chrysalis.

After hanging upside down for nearly two weeks, the chrysalises began to shake. They shook and shook until their cases opened.

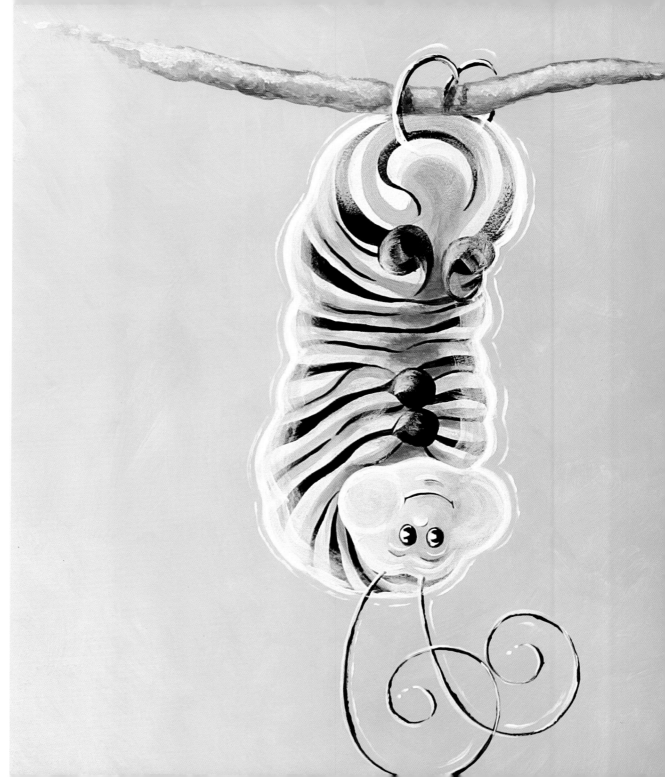

Out came three beautiful butterflies.

The new butterflies stretched out their wings. Then they practiced flying.

"Look at all the beautiful flowers," said Koa Butterfly.

"All kinds," said Monarch Butterfly.

"Let's all drink nectar from our favorites," said Lepe-o-Hina Butterfly.

"Wait—what is all that noise?" said Monarch Butterfly.

The three friends looked
around and saw three brand-new
caterpillars.

"I know which leaves are best
to eat," said one of the caterpillars.

"No, I do!" said each of the
others.

"Young caterpillars," said Koa
Butterfly, "you need the spirit of
aloha to survive in this forest."

"*Aloha*?" said the little
caterpillars.

"Yes," said Monarch. "Think
with your heart and you will
understand *aloha*."

Lepe-o-Hina Butterfly smiled. "When we live with *aloha*, beautiful things happen."

The Butterfly Life Cycle

Lepe-o-Hina and *koa* butterflies are native to Hawaiʻi. The monarch butterfly has been in Hawaiʻi since the 1850s. *Pulelehua* is another name for the *lepe-o-Hina* butterfly. It is also the general Hawaiian word for butterfly.

There are four stages in the butterfly life cycle: egg, caterpillar, chrysalis, and butterfly. The process of changing from one form to the next is called **metamorphosis**.

Egg Stage
Butterflies lay their eggs on leaves. The eggs rest on their leaves for about one week. Then they hatch.

Caterpillar Stage
When the egg hatches, a caterpillar crawls out. The caterpillar's hard outer shell is called an **exoskeleton**.

Chrysalis Stage

After about two weeks, a caterpillar becomes a **chrysalis**. While it hangs upside down on a branch, its body changes inside.

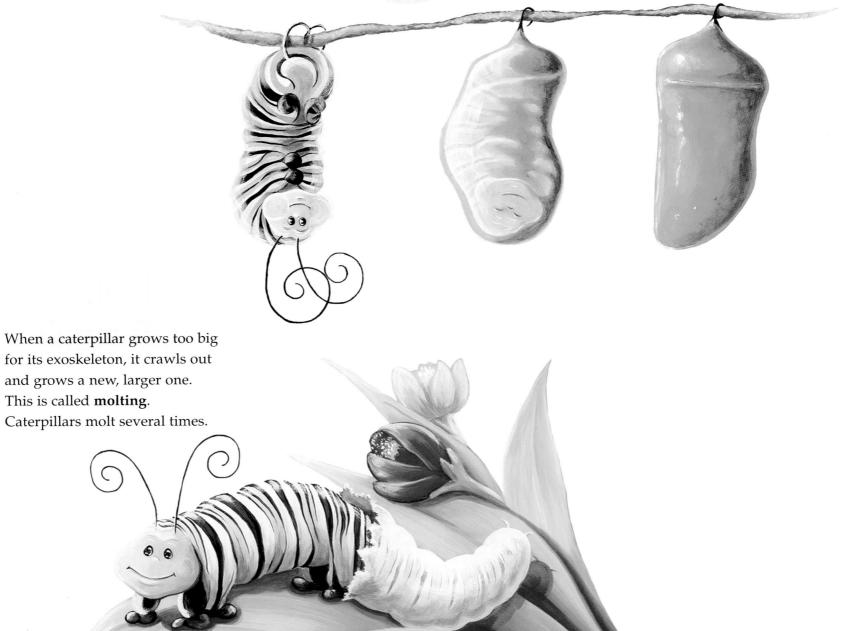

When a caterpillar grows too big for its exoskeleton, it crawls out and grows a new, larger one. This is called **molting**. Caterpillars molt several times.

Butterfly Stage

After about two weeks, a butterfly emerges from the chrysalis. It drinks nectar from flowers and helps more plants to grow. This is called **pollination**. The butterfly also lays eggs. Then, the life cycle begins again.

A butterfly's delicate and beautiful ways

are reminders of the **aloha** *in all of our hearts.*